Disney

Pocahontas

Ladybird

CHAPTER ONE

It began in old London town in the year 1607.

Early one foggy morning, the docks were bustling with men loading cargo. The English sailing ship, the *Susan Constant*, was about to get under way. She would be carrying daring adventurers on a voyage far across the sea, all the way to Virginia in America. America was the New World and the men hoped to find plenty of gold and jewels there.

Thomas' whole family had gathered to say goodbye and wish him well.

"Godspeed, laddie," said his father, shaking his hand.

"My dear boy, take care of yourself," his mother told him. She tried hard to hold back her tears.

His little sister tugged at his sleeve. "Watch out for the Indians!" she warned him.

Thomas' mother began to sob.

"Don't worry, Mother," he said, hugging her. "I'll be all right." His eyes were shining brightly. "I'm off on a *great* adventure!"

Disney

POCAHONTAS

Ladybird books are widely available, but in case of difficulty may be ordered by post or telephone from:
Ladybird Books – Cash Sales Department Littlegate Road Paignton Devon TQ3 3BE Telephone 01803 554761

A catalogue record for this book is available from the British Library

Published by Ladybird Books Ltd Loughborough Leicestershire UK
LADYBIRD and the device of a Ladybird are trademarks of Ladybird Books Ltd

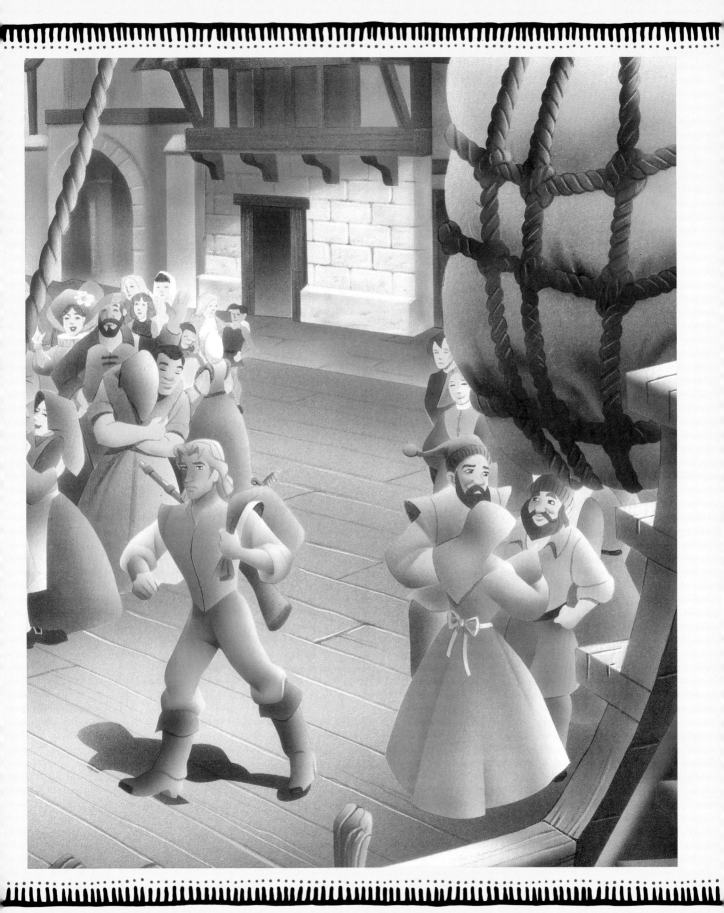

Not far from Thomas, another young man headed towards the ship. He was tall, with golden hair, and he carried a musket on his back.

Alone, without any well-wishers to see him off, he strode onto the dock and quickly stepped onto a cannon being hoisted aboard ship.

Two men stood at the ship's railing and watched as the cannon was lowered onto the deck. Lon, the shorter of the two men, gaped in surprise.

"Ben, look!" he said, eagerly nudging his companion. "Isn't that Smith?"

"It sure is," answered Ben. "That's a real sea dog if ever there was one!" Overhearing the conversation, Thomas quickly made his way over to Lon and Ben.

"Did you say Smith? Captain John Smith?" said Thomas. "I've heard some amazing stories about him. Is he really coming on this voyage with us?"

Ben rolled his eyes at Thomas' ignorance.

"Don't be a fool," he told him. "Of course he's coming. You can't fight the Indians without John Smith!"

Smith overheard Ben and smiled. "That's right," he said. "I'm not about to let you boys have all the fun."

On the dockside, the crowd roared as a shining gilt carriage pulled up.

One of Thomas' brothers pointed to the carriage. "Look at that!" he shouted as the team of high-spirited horses pranced up to the ship. "Must belong to somebody rich."

"Hush, lovey, mind your manners," said his mother. "That's John Ratcliffe, the Lord Governor. He's in charge of the expedition."

Governor Ratcliffe puffed as he stepped out of the carriage, then paused to catch his breath. His attendant, Wiggins, hopped out of the coach right behind him, carefully carrying a little pug dog on a satin pillow.

The Governor strutted through the crowd with his nose in the air. The little pug dog, called Percy, followed his master up the gangplank, his snout high in the air as well.

On deck a young man hoisted a flag. It fluttered in the brisk wind.

"All hands on board!" he shouted.

Thomas' family waved their final goodbyes as the crew slipped the mooring ropes from the dock. The *Susan Constant* was under way at last. As the ship headed downriver, the departing men waved back to their friends and relations. Only one man did not. With his musket still slung on his back, John Smith faced the open sea.

*   *   *

For weeks the ship rolled through calm waters, but one night the wind quickened. The huge sails billowed out and the ship charged through the tumbling waves. Lightning cracked and flashed. With thunder booming in their ears, the men struggled to keep the ship on course.

"Cut her speed!" shouted one sailor. "Furl the sails!"

High above, Smith swung from rope to rope helping to secure the ship's rigging. Thomas, with panic rising in his voice, yelled up to him, "Smith! The cannons are breaking loose!"

Smith swung down from the mast and landed next to Thomas.

"Reef the topsails!" he shouted to the men. "Steady on your course." He looked down at Thomas. "It's all right," he said. "We'll get them tied down. Don't you wor…"

The deck heaved as a gigantic wave exploded over the rail.

"Thomas!" shouted Smith. "Watch out!"

But his warning came too late. The wave sent Thomas sprawling across the deck, over the rail and into the ocean.

"Man overboard!" shouted one of the men.

"Help!" Thomas yelled, thrashing about in the foaming water.

"We'll never be able to save him!" shouted Ben. "He's lost!"

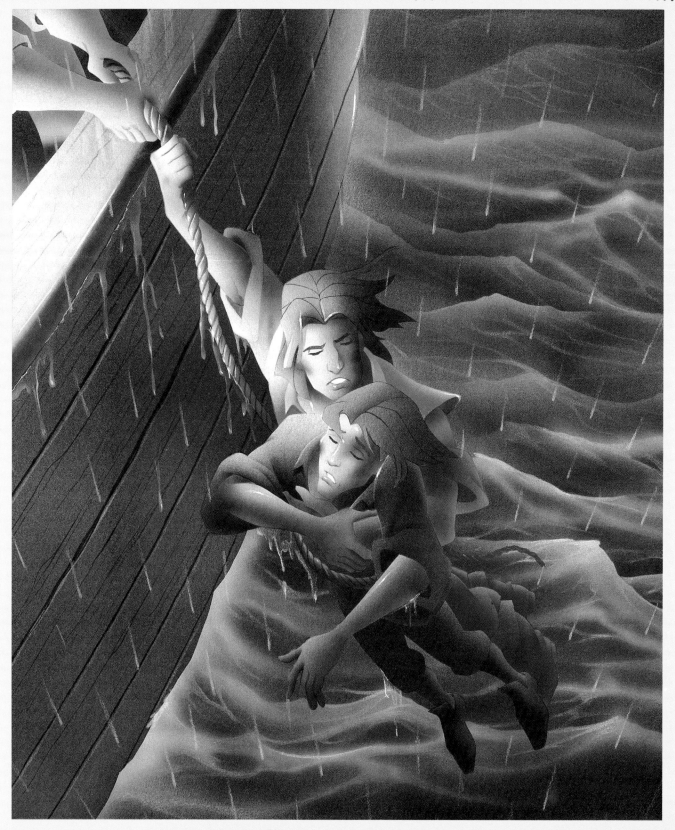

"Help!" Thomas cried out again.

As the horrified men watched, Thomas was carried further and further away from the ship.

Smith hastily tied the end of a rope round his waist. Then he dived over the rail.

"Smith!" shouted Ben. "Are you crazy?"

With steady, powerful strokes, Smith swam through the rolling waves. He reached out and grabbed Thomas.

"Hang on, I've got you!" he said, wrapping one arm round Thomas.

The men on board began to pull on the rope tied to Smith's waist.

"Harder!" Lon shouted to them. "Put your backs into it!"

Fighting against the strength of the sea, the men slowly hauled in Smith and Thomas. Straining every muscle, the men pulled them both alongside the ship and then hoisted them over the rail.

Smith and Thomas lay flat on the deck, gasping for air. The other men silently gathered round.

A few moments later, Smith blew a stream of water out of his mouth. "That was refreshing," he said.

"Well done, Smith," said Lon. His eyes glistened with tears of relief.

"Of course," Smith said, looking at Ben, "I expect you'd do the same for me."

Ben gulped. "Of course I would, sir," he stammered. "Any time!"

"Trouble on deck?" asked Governor Ratcliffe, coming out of his cabin. Wiggins teetered behind, trying to hold an umbrella over his master's head.

"Thomas fell overboard, sir," Smith answered him.

Thomas struggled to his feet. "Smith rescued me, sir."

"Thank heavens you've been successfully retrieved. Good job, Smith," the Governor said, eyeing both men.

Then he raised his voice for everyone to hear.

"Don't lose heart, men! It won't be long before we reach the New World," he told them. "Just remember what awaits us – freedom! Riches! Gold!"

Ratcliffe struggled to keep his balance in the whipping wind.

"You are the finest crew our nation has to offer," he shouted. "And nothing, not wind or rain – not even a thousand Indians – shall stand in our way!"

The Governor turned back towards his cabin where it was warm and dry. Wiggins stumbled alongside, still struggling with the umbrella.

"That was a stirring oration, sir," he said, opening the cabin door for Ratcliffe.

Governor Ratcliffe grinned.

"Let us hope so," he answered under his breath. "I'll need those witless peasants to dig up my gold!"

* * *

Thomas smiled at Smith. "This New World's going to be great. I'll get rich and build myself a big house. And if any Indian tries to stop me – I'll shoot him!"

Smith smiled back. "Just worry about that fortune of yours, Thomas. Leave the Indians to me."

"Do you really think they'll give us much trouble?" Thomas asked.

Ben picked up Thomas' dripping hat and handed it to him.

"Not as much trouble as Smith'll give *them*!" he said.

Thomas wrung out his hat. "I never realised the voyage would be so hard."

Smith grinned. "You should have seen my *last* voyage!"

"Why do you keep doing this time and time again?" asked Thomas.

Smith looked out towards the horizon. The storm had passed and the first light of dawn was brightening the sea.

"I don't know," he answered. "I suppose I just never found a reason to stop."

CHAPTER TWO

ar across the ocean, a wide river wound through a wooded land. Along its reedy shallows, marsh birds probed for tiny crabs.

Further out, bluefish and flounder swam. In the deepest waters dwelt the giant sturgeon, each one as heavy as a small boat.

A village lay in the shady forest alongside the river. In its centre stood a circle of wooden posts, each one carved with a face. Here, the villagers often held dances.

The dwellings were made from poles and woven mats. They rested beneath the trees like big overturned bowls.

One day, the village women were out in the field picking vegetables, beans and corn. Not far away, other forest dwellers were also gathering gifts from the generous land. At the edge of the forest, white-tailed deer browsed on ferns and grass and in the thorny thicket, birds and black bears nibbled on nuts and juicy berries.

Two small children dashed from the river into the field.

"The warriors are coming home!" they called out, excitedly.

The women dropped their baskets and ran to the water's edge.

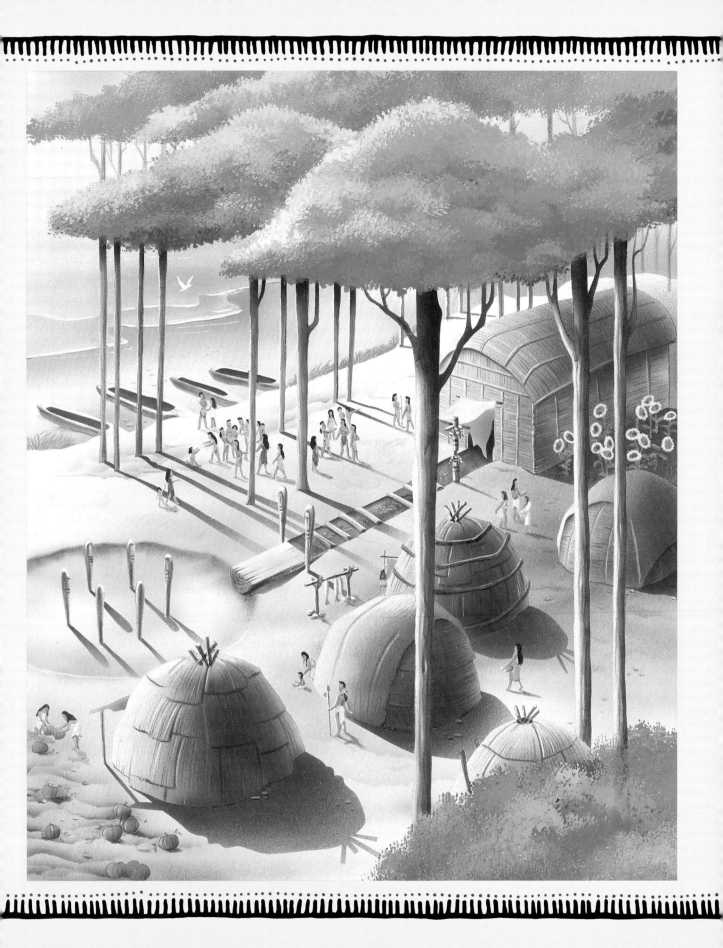

Kekata, the tribal medicine man, was already there waiting patiently. As the warriors beached their canoes, he stepped forward to welcome the Chief.

"Chief Powhatan," he said. "We have received word of your victory. Your return has brought joy to the village. Look at all the smiling faces."

Chief Powhatan looked over the small crowd. "There is one smiling face I do not see," he said. "Where is my daughter?"

"You know Pocahontas," Kekata answered with a smile. "She goes wherever the wind takes her. But don't worry, I sent Nakoma after her."

*　　*　　*

Nakoma paddled along the shoreline looking for Pocahontas. Finally, she looked up and spotted her friend at the edge of a high cliff. With the wind ruffling her hair, Pocahontas stood gazing across the land and water that stretched before her.

As always, Pocahontas' companion, Meeko the raccoon, was at her heels. Hovering close to Pocahontas' shoulder was another friend, a tiny hummingbird called Flit. Pocahontas saw Nakoma and waved to her.

"Your father's back!" Nakoma called. "Come down here!"

Pocahontas stood poised on the edge of the cliff. Slowly she raised her arms.

"No! Not that way!" Nakoma cried out.

Pocahontas hardly made a splash as she dived gracefully into the river.

Nervously, Nakoma peered down into the water.

"Pocahontas?" she said. "Pocahontas? You'd better be all right, because I'm not…"

Suddenly, the canoe tipped over and Nakoma was thrown headfirst into the water.

"Pocahontas!" she laughed as her smiling friend bobbed up next to her from under the overturned canoe. "Don't you think we're getting a little old for these games? What were you doing up there?"

"Thinking," said Pocahontas.

"About that dream again?" asked Nakoma.

"I know it means something," said Pocahontas. "I just don't know what."

"Well," said Nakoma, "now that your father's back, you should ask him about it."

Pocahontas smiled. "Maybe I should."

*　　*　　*

Pocahontas and Nakoma paddled back home. As they pulled the canoe up onto the shore, Chief Powhatan was speaking to the excited villagers.

"*Chesk-cham-ay!* My friends!" said the Chief. "The Massawomecks are defeated. Our village is safe again."

He turned to a young warrior standing close by.

"Our warriors fought with courage," he told his people, "but none as bravely as Kocoum. Tonight we will feast in his honour."

As the crowd cheered, the young warrior stood grim-faced and still as stone.

"Kocoum is very handsome," Nakoma whispered to Pocahontas.

"I especially love the smile," Pocahontas whispered back.

She started walking towards her father. She felt proud and happy as she pressed her way through the crowd. Chief Powhatan was loved and respected and Pocahontas knew she was closest to his heart.

Chief Powhatan smiled when he saw Pocahontas. He held out his arms. "My daughter," he said.

"Father!" said Pocahontas, holding him close to her. "I'm so glad you've come home safely."

"Come with me," said Chief Powhatan. "Let us walk together. Tell me what you have been doing."

"Father," Pocahontas told him, "something has happened lately that I do not understand."

Chief Powhatan touched her gently on the shoulder. "I am here to listen."

"For many nights now," Pocahontas explained, "I've been having the same dream. I think it is telling me that something is about to happen. Something exciting."

Her father smiled at her.

"You are right, my dear daughter," he said. "Something exciting *is* about to happen."

"Really?" asked Pocahontas. "What is it?"

With great pride in his voice, Chief Powhatan told her, "Kocoum has asked for your hand in marriage."

Pocahontas was shocked. Marry Kocoum?

"But Father," she said, "Kocoum is always so... *serious*."

"He is my bravest warrior, Pocahontas," said Chief Powhatan. "I told him if he were your husband, it would make my heart soar."

Pocahontas tried to explain her wishes.

"I think my dream is telling me something else," she said. "I think it's pointing me down another path."

Chief Powhatan shook his head sternly.

"*This* is the right path for you," he told her. "You are the daughter of a chief. It is time to take your place among our people."

"But Father," said Pocahontas. "Why can't I..."

"You have your mother's spirit and independence, Pocahontas," her father said. "You guide your canoe with ease through the roughest waters. You follow tracks through the forest as well as any of my warriors. You do many things on your own." He looked at his daughter fondly.

17

"But even the wild mountain stream must some day join the big river, my daughter," he continued. "Rivers are steady – steady as the beating drum. Steadiness is good for people too."

He placed a necklace round Pocahontas' neck. Hanging from it was a smooth shell.

"Your mother wore this for our wedding," he said. "It was her great wish that you would wear it at your own."

Chief Powhatan stepped back and looked at it. "It suits you," he said, looking pleased.

Then he walked away, leaving Pocahontas alone with her thoughts.

Pocahontas sat down by the river bank. Meeko ambled to her side and Flit hovered over the flowers nearby.

Pocahontas thought about what her father had said. She had always followed his wishes, but this time it was different. She did not want to marry Kocoum.

As Pocahontas stared into the flowing river, Meeko sat quietly pawing at the water. Suddenly a frog popped up right under his nose. Meeko jumped back in surprise and scrambled onto Pocahontas' shoulder.

"See!" laughed Pocahontas. "Rivers aren't steady at all. They're always changing."

And who wants to be steady anyway? she thought to herself.

CHAPTER THREE

ocahontas pushed her canoe into the water and picked up Meeko, who was hunting about for more frogs.

"Come along," she said. "Maybe Grandmother Willow will tell me what to do."

Whirring frantically, Flit darted out from the trees.

Pocahontas laughed. "Don't worry," she said. "We wouldn't leave you behind."

Pocahontas paddled along a winding stream that flowed into the heart of the forest. Then she floated into a secluded glade. And there, as always, Grandmother Willow was patiently waiting. For hundreds of years she had stood there—her deep roots drawing water from the stream and her long, trailing leaves breathing life from the sun.

Pocahontas climbed out of her canoe and sat quietly on a large stump in front of Grandmother Willow.

"Grandmother Willow," she said, "I need to talk to you."

The bark on the ancient tree began to change shape. The face of an old woman appeared.

"Good morning, child," said Grandmother Willow, her gentle voice filling the air. "I was hoping you'd visit me today. Why, you're wearing your mother's necklace!"

"That's what I want to speak to you about," said Pocahontas. "My father wishes me to marry Kocoum."

"Kocoum?" said Grandmother Willow. Her face crumpled into a frown. "But he's so… serious."

"I know," said Pocahontas. "Father thinks it's the right path for me." She stroked Meeko's back. "But there's something else. Lately, I've been having a strange dream."

"Oh, good!" exclaimed Grandmother Willow. "You know how I love dreams! Tell me *all* about it."

"I dream," Pocahontas began, "that I am running through the forest. Then, right there before me is an arrow. As I look at it, it begins to spin."

"A spinning arrow," said Grandmother Willow. "How unusual."

"Yes," agreed Pocahontas. "It spins faster and faster until suddenly it stops."

"And then?" asked Grandmother Willow.

Pocahontas shrugged her shoulders. "And then I wake up."

Grandmother Willow was silent for several minutes.

"Hmmm," she said, thoughtfully. "Hmmm," she said again.

Finally she spoke.

"Child," said Grandmother Willow, "it seems to me this spinning arrow is pointing you down your path."

"I know," said Pocahontas. "But what *is* my path? How am I ever going to find it?"

Grandmother Willow chuckled softly to herself.

"Your mother asked me the very same question."

"What did you tell her?" asked Pocahontas.

"I told her to listen. All around you are spirits. They live in the earth, the water and the sky. Listen to them and they will guide you."

A light breeze rustled through Grandmother Willow's leaves.

"I can hear the wind," said Pocahontas.

"What is it telling you?" asked Grandmother Willow.

Pocahontas listened, quietly. Then she sighed. "I don't know."

"There is more than listening with your ears," said Grandmother Willow. "You must also listen with your heart. Then you will understand."

Pocahontas closed her eyes and listened again. After a minute or two, her eyes opened wide.

"The wind *is* saying something!" Pocahontas cried. "It says something is coming." Then she looked confused. *"Strange clouds?"*

"What is it?" asked Grandmother Willow.

"The wind is telling me to climb to the top of you!" said Pocahontas.

"Well," said Grandmother Willow, "you'd better get going!"

Pulling herself up from branch to branch, Pocahontas climbed to the top of the tree.

"What do you see?" asked Grandmother Willow.

"Clouds!" answered Pocahontas.

She sucked in her breath. *"Strange clouds."*

In the distance, the huge white sails of the *Susan Constant* billowed above the treetops.

* * *

Aboard the *Susan Constant*, Governor Ratcliffe flung open a porthole. He gaped at the forest that lined the coast.

"Look at it, Wiggins," he said. "An entire New World crammed full of gold, just waiting for *me*."

Wiggins was serving Percy his dinner. The stout little dog sniffed the steaming food. After he inspected it, he held up his jowly chin.

"We'll have scores of adventures too, won't we, Percy?" Wiggins said.

Percy ignored him and nibbled his dinner.

"Do you think we'll meet some Indians?" Wiggins asked Ratcliffe.

"If we do," said the Governor, "we shall be sure to give them a proper greeting."

"Bang! Bang!" said Wiggins, picking up a large spoon and pointing it like a gun. "I do love a fracas!"

Just then, John Smith poked his head round the cabin door.

"This is a perfect place to anchor, Governor!" he exclaimed. "The water's deep enough. We can pull up close to shore."

"Well then, give the order for the landing boats," said Ratcliffe. "Oh, about the natives. I'm counting on you to make sure they don't disrupt our mission."

"Don't worry, sir," said Smith. "If they're anything like the ones I've fought before, it's nothing I can't handle." He smiled, gave a quick salute and left.

Governor Ratcliffe frowned.

"The men like Smith, don't they?" he said to Wiggins.

"Don't worry, sir," said Wiggins. "Once they get to know you, I'm sure they'll like you too."

"Well, I don't give a hoot if they like me or not!" said Ratcliffe. "When King James sees all the gold I bring back, success will be *mine* at last!"

*   *   *

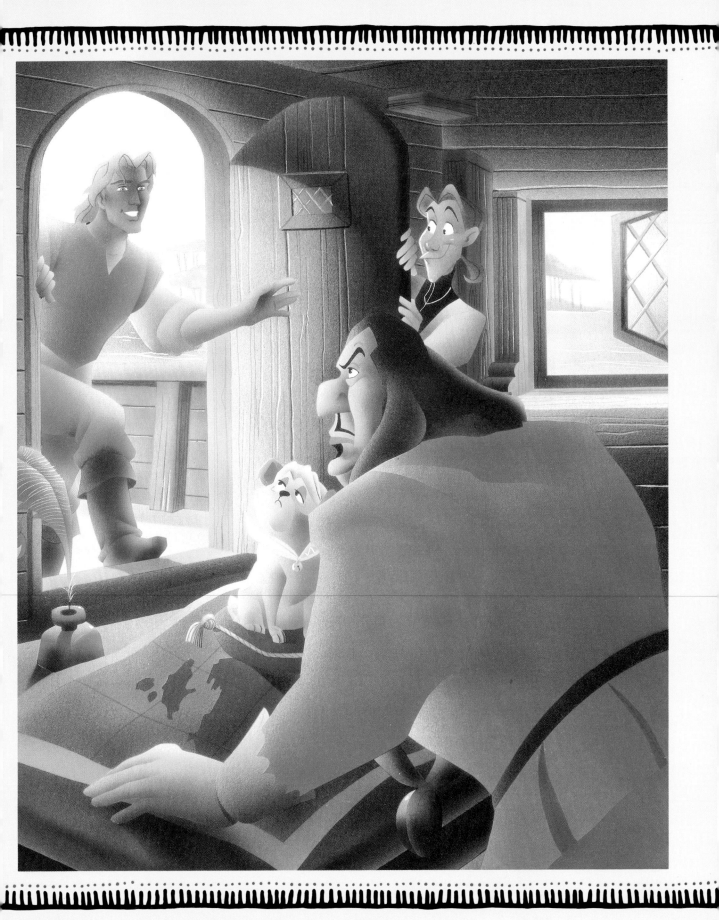

John Smith climbed from a rowing boat onto the pebbly shore. He stared up at the forest of towering trees. They were the tallest trees he'd ever seen.

"I've never seen anything like it," said Thomas, who had accompanied Smith. "And to think — it all belongs to us!"

Smith strode across the shore and pulled himself up into the branches of a tall pine tree.

"Smith," Thomas called up to him, "what are you doing?"

"Getting a better look," Smith answered, climbing higher and higher. He gazed at the river and land that spread out beneath him.

Not far away, Pocahontas was also trying to get a better look. Hiding behind a bush on a rocky ledge, she watched Smith climb the tree.

Meeko leaned out over the ledge.

"Shh," Pocahontas whispered, trying to hold on to him. The man was climbing right towards them! Meeko wriggled out of her grasp.

Smith stopped climbing. What was that rustling sound on the cliff? He grabbed the knife from inside his boot.

Pocahontas held her breath.

"Will you look at this," Smith said to himself, sticking the knife back into his boot. He reached out and picked up the curious raccoon. "You're a strange-looking fellow."

Meeko sniffed at the leather pouch tied to Smith's belt.

Smith reached inside and pulled out a biscuit.

"You hungry?" he asked. "Here you go. It's a biscuit. It's food. Well, sort of."

Meeko grabbed the biscuit and gobbled it up.

"You like it, eh!" said Smith. "But just try eating it for four months!"

Pocahontas smiled with relief. The man was not going to hurt Meeko. In fact, he seemed kind. Pocahontas leaned further out for a better look.

Meeko picked up some crumbs from the ground. After he had eaten them he looked towards Pocahontas.

Smith glanced over at the ledge. "Have you got a friend back there?" he asked.

Pocahontas held her breath and leaned back as far as she could. The man was practically staring straight at her!

Humming frantically, Flit burst out of the shadows and dived at Smith's head.

Smith flung out his arm to protect himself. Again and again Flit whirled straight at him. Then Thomas called from the shore.

"Smith, you'd better get down here. The Governor is coming ashore."

"All right, all right," Smith said to Flit. "I'm leaving."

As he climbed down the tree, Pocahontas gave a sigh of relief. That had been too close!

Pocahontas stared down at the *Susan Constant*. She couldn't wait to tell Nakoma about her adventure—and about the strange-looking man who liked to climb trees!

CHAPTER FOUR

he Indian village council called a hasty meeting.

"I saw them from the ridge," said one warrior. "They're starting to come ashore! They have hair on their faces—like dogs! And did you see their skin? It's pale and sickly."

Another warrior spoke up. "I have never seen such a boat. It must come from the Great Waters."

Chief Powhatan raised his hand and the room fell silent.

"My brothers," he told them, "we must know more about these visitors."

He turned to the village medicine man. "Kekata," he said, "tell us what you see."

Kekata poured a handful of powder on the fire. A plume of smoke rose from the flames. As it changed shape, he studied it.

"These men are not like us," he said. "They prowl the earth like wolves, consuming everything in their path. And their weapons spout fire and thunder!"

Kocoum rose to his feet.

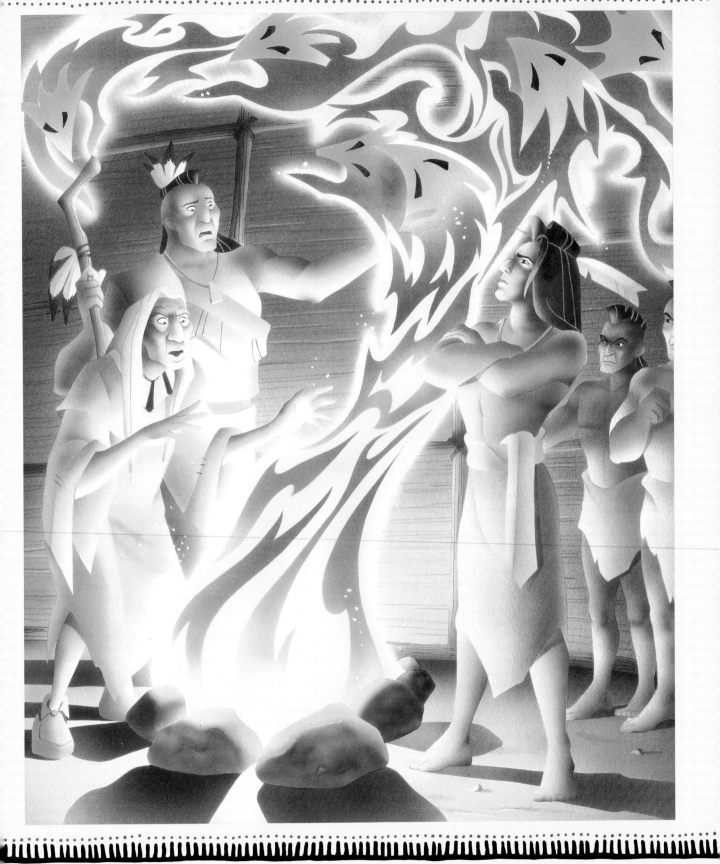

"Great Powhatan," he said, "I will lead our warriors to the river and attack. We will destroy these invaders!"

Noisily, the rest of the warriors agreed.

"Kocoum," said Chief Powhatan, speaking firmly. "In past battles, we knew our enemy. But these pale visitors are strange to us. Take some men to the river to observe them."

Then he spoke to the assembled villagers, "Let us hope they do not intend to stay."

* * *

Down at the shore another meeting was being held.

Governor Ratcliffe, clutching a flag high in one hand, loudly declared, "I hereby claim this land and all its riches in the name of His Majesty, King James, and do so name this settlement—Jamestown!"

He jammed the flagpole into the ground.

"Well," he said, turning to Smith, "it appears I've selected the perfect location. Not a native in sight."

"Sir," said Smith, "just because we don't see them doesn't mean they're not out there."

"Perhaps, then," suggested Ratcliffe, "you should venture forth and determine their whereabouts?"

"Yes, sir," said Smith, grabbing his musket. "If there are any Indians out there, I'll find them!"

"Fine," said Ratcliffe. "And while you're gone, the rest of the men will break out the spades and start digging. Let's not forget what the Spanish found when they came to the New World. *Gold*! Mountains of it!"

As Smith headed into the forest, he could hear the men singing loudly as they dug for gold.

Later that day, deep in the forest, Smith stopped at the edge of a waterfall. He cupped his hands in the icy water. But as he leaned forward to drink, a reflection caught his eye. Someone was behind him.

Smith spun round. He was all alone. But he trusted his instincts—someone was definitely watching him. He leapt across the stream and disappeared behind the falls where he waited. Then, with his musket ready to fire, Smith leapt out onto a rock and took careful aim—and could hardly believe what he saw. It was a young woman. She had dark eyes and her long black hair shone in the dappled light. She was the most beautiful woman Smith had ever seen. Instantly, he lowered his musket.

Pocahontas stood, equally shocked and still, except for the wind that blew her hair across her face. She was staring back at the man who'd been in the tree—the man with yellow hair that glinted like sunlight and eyes as blue as a robin's egg.

Slowly, Smith removed his helmet and stepped towards Pocahontas.

"It's all right," he said. "I'm not going to hurt you."

But his movement and voice were enough to break the trance that had held Pocahontas there. She quickly turned and ran.

"No, wait, please," he called after her. "Don't run off."

Pocahontas ran to the river bank, thankful that her canoe was in sight. Just as she stepped in and was about to push off, she heard Smith's voice again. Pocahontas hesitated for a moment and looked back. The man's voice was kind. And after all, he'd been very gentle with Meeko.

Smith caught up with her and offered his hand.

"Here," he said, "let me help you out of there."

Pocahontas stood facing him.

"Who are you?" Smith whispered.

"*Mat-ta-que-nat-o-rath* (I do not understand)," said Pocahontas.

32

How foolish of me, Smith thought. *She doesn't understand what I'm saying!*

A slight breeze sprang up and swirled about them. Pocahontas gasped. The wind was speaking to her. It was carrying Grandmother Willow's words!

> *Listen with your heart,*
> *Then you will understand.*

Pocahontas pointed to herself.

"Pocahontas," she said to the man. "My name is Pocahontas."

Smith smiled. So she *did* understand him.

"My name is John Smith," he said, pointing to himself.

Pocahontas took Smith's outstretched hand and together they walked through the forest.

CHAPTER FIVE

t the edge of a clearing, hidden behind a gooseberry bush, Kocoum spied on the white men.

His comrade, Namontack, silently crept up behind him.

"There are thirty more down by the ridge," he whispered.

"That makes more than one hundred," said Kocoum. "Look at them. First they cut down the trees. Then they push sticks deep into the ground! What do they wish to find?"

As he spoke, there was a loud CRACK in the distance. Then the ground shuddered beneath their feet.

Namontack's eyes shone with anger.

"Another tree has fallen," he said.

"I wish we knew what they were saying," said Kocoum. "That fat one over there – the one eating – I think he is their chief."

*　*　*

Governor Ratcliffe, holding a plate, gnawed noisily on a greasy chicken leg.

"That's it, that's it, keep at it, men!" he called out. "Keep digging. The gold's got to be here somewhere!"

He looked at the chicken on his plate.

"Where's Wiggins?" he roared.

"Right here, sir," answered Wiggins, appearing instantly at his side.

"Dispose of this!" Ratcliffe ordered, handing him the plate.

"Perhaps Percy would like to nibble on one of the bones," suggested Wiggins. "Fetch!" he told the little dog, throwing a bone into the gooseberry bush at the edge of the clearing.

Percy scrambled after the bone—and raced straight into Kocoum and Namontack! Startled, he yelped and leapt high into the air. The warriors, equally surprised, jumped to their feet too.

"What's happened to my poor Percy?" Ratcliffe shouted. Then he saw Kocoum and Namontack.

"It's an ambush!" he screamed. "Men, arm yourselves!"

Thomas and the others quickly scrambled to find their muskets.

"Where's Smith when I need him?" Ratcliffe cried. Grabbing a musket, he took aim and fired.

The blast caught Namontack's leg. Clutching the wound, the warrior fell to the ground.

"Namontack!" cried Kocoum. He raced to help his friend.

One of the settlers sprang from the bushes ready to club Kocoum with the butt of his rifle.

Kocoum wrestled him to the ground. He struck at the man's chest with his stone knife, but the blade simply snapped off. He saw that the man's chest was protected by a hard, shiny plate.

38

As more white men headed towards him Kocoum was overcome by a fear he had never known. For the first time, he felt defenceless. *How could his people fight these pale strangers?* he thought. *These men wore clothing that shattered stone. And Kekata was right—their weapons exploded like thunder and lightning!*

Horrified, Kocoum knew that he could do nothing but flee. He hoisted his injured friend over his shoulder and quickly retreated.

* * *

Chief Powhatan knelt beside Namontack as Kekata tended the terrible wound. The medicine man sadly shook his head.

"This wound is strange to me," he said.

Rage boiled within Chief Powhatan.

"They invade our shore and destroy our land," he said. He stared at the wounded man. "Now this!"

Chief Powhatan rose and spoke with Kocoum.

"We will fight this enemy," he said. "Send messengers to every village in our nation. We will call on our brothers to help us."

Then Chief Powhatan addressed the villagers.

"*No one* is to go near the white men," he ordered. "These creatures who come from the Great Waters—they are savages!"

CHAPTER SIX

Pocahontas sat at the edge of the river with Meeko and Flit nearby.

Sitting down on the grass beside her, Smith asked, "Where do you live?"

"My village is on the Chicahominy," Pocahontas answered.

"Chica-hominy?" asked Smith.

"It's a river," explained Pocahontas. "It flows into this river—the Quiyoughcohannock."

Smith shook his head in wonder. "You have the most unusual names here… Chicahominy… Quiyoughcohannock… Pocahontas."

"Your name is unusual too," Pocahontas told him. "John Smith. What does it mean?"

"It's just a name," replied Smith.

Pocahontas was surprised. "How strange. All our names mean something."

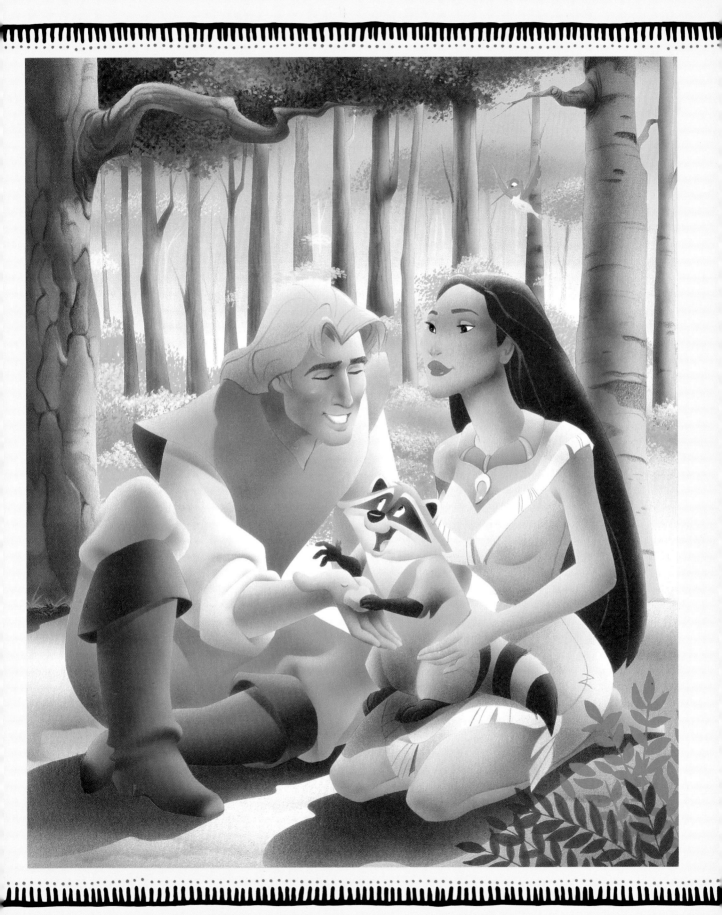

"And what does Pocahontas mean?" Smith asked her.

Pocahontas grinned. "'Little Mischief'," she said.

"And this is Meeko," she said, patting the little raccoon.

Smith hid his surprise. This looked like the same animal he had given the biscuit to.

He held out his hand. "How do you do, Meeko?" he said.

Pocahontas looked confused.

"It's all right," explained Smith. "It's just a handshake. Let me show you."

He shook Pocahontas' hand. "It's how we say hello."

Pocahontas smiled. "This is how *we* say hello." She held her hand up, palm facing outwards, and moved it in a circle in the air.

"*Wing-gap-o*," she said.

Smith copied her. "*Wing-gap-o*."

Then Pocahontas moved her hand in a circle back the other way. "And this is how we say goodbye."

Smith grinned and put his hand up against hers. "I'd rather stay with hello!"

Buzzing importantly, Flit landed on Pocahontas' shoulder and shook his beak at Smith.

"Flit doesn't like strangers," Pocahontas explained.

Smith held out his finger and tried to coax Flit to hop onto it.

"But I'm not a stranger any more, am I, Flit?" he asked the hummingbird.

Flit turned his beak away.

Smith laughed. "Stubborn little fellow, isn't he?"

Pocahontas nodded and smiled. "*Very* stubborn."

Meeko began to sniff the air.

"Here," said Smith. He untied the leather pouch that hung from his belt and took out a biscuit. "I know what he…" Meeko snatched the biscuit and gobbled it up, "…wants," finished Smith.

Hunting for more food, Meeko grabbed the leather pouch and poked his head inside. But instead of finding another biscuit, he reappeared with a compass clasped between his teeth. Growling with delight, he carried it up the nearest tree.

"Meeko, come back with that," scolded Pocahontas. "It doesn't belong to you!"

"Oh, it's all right," said Smith. "He can keep it."

"What was it?" Pocahontas asked.

"Just my compass," said Smith.

"Compass?" asked Pocahontas.

"It tells you how to find your way when you get lost," Smith explained to her. "But it's all right. I can always buy another one when I get back to London."

"London?" asked Pocahontas. "Is that your village?"

"Yes," said Smith. "A very *big* village."

"What is it like?"

"Oh," said Smith, "it has streets filled with carriages, bridges over the rivers, buildings as tall as trees…"

Pocahontas' eyes grew round. "I'd like to see those things."

Smith smiled at her. "You will."

"How?" asked Pocahontas, very surprised.

"We're going to build them here," said Smith. "We'll show the people of your village how to use this land properly. How to make the most of it."

"Make the most of it?" asked Pocahontas.

"Yes," said Smith, "we'll build roads and decent houses…"

Pocahontas jumped to her feet.

"Our houses are *fine!*" she said. With that, she walked down the river bank and climbed back into her canoe.

"Wait a minute," said Smith, holding the end of the canoe.

"Let go," said Pocahontas.

"You think your houses are fine only because you don't know any better," Smith went on. "There's so much we can teach you. We've improved the lives of savages all over the world."

Pocahontas was stunned. *"Savages!"*

Smith tried to explain. "It's just a word. You know, a term for people who are uncivilised."

"Like me?" asked Pocahontas, not hiding her anger.

"Well," stumbled Smith. "When I say *uncivilised*, what I mean is…"

Pocahontas climbed out of her canoe and finished the sentence for him. "What you mean is," she said, poking him in the chest, "not like *you!*" She looked hard into Smith's eyes. "You think your people know everything. But my people know this land as yours never will. The creatures of the forest, each rock and every bird, the fish in the waters – they are our brothers and sisters. We all live together. We are all one – with the sun, the moon and the stars."

Smith listened to what Pocahontas had to say. He followed her further into the forest, more and more drawn by her words. After a while, they rested by a little stream. A leaf drifted down and landed in the water. Pocahontas handed it to Smith.

"Even this little leaf has a spirit and a name."

Smith smiled, doubtfully.

"Do you not see?" she continued. "You, me, Meeko and Flit, the rainstorms and mountain tops—we are all a part of the earth. We are joined to one another."

Pocahontas formed a circle with her arms. "My people say life on earth is like a giant circle. It has no beginning and it has no end. I think your people do not understand the earth. They think it is a dead thing."

As Pocahontas spoke, Smith felt a change come over him. He had never known anyone so at home in their own world. What she was saying made sense. He looked at her with a new understanding.

* * *

For the rest of the afternoon they talked and enjoyed the beautiful day. Smith saw bears playing with their cubs and an eagle fly to its nest high atop an old tree.

Pocahontas' anger had quickly disappeared. She felt happy and peaceful as she pointed out brilliant sunflowers and other plants and animals to Smith.

Later in the day, as the sky turned a blazing pink, the two gazed into each other's eyes for what seemed like a very long time.

But then Pocahontas suddenly looked away.

"What is it?" Smith asked.

"The drums," said Pocahontas. "They mean trouble. Something is happening in the village. I have to go."

Smith pulled Pocahontas close. "Will I see you again?"

Pocahontas had never felt so confused. Here was a man who had insulted her people and yet she liked him – very much.

"I shouldn't be here," she said.

"I want to see you again," said Smith.

"I have to go," Pocahontas whispered.

Feeling both happy and sad, she ran home.

CHAPTER SEVEN

he next morning was rainy. Smith watched in silence as Lon and Ben raised another section of the fort wall.

Thomas appeared, lugging a heavy plank. "Think this'll keep the natives out?" he asked. "This stockade will close in the whole settlement."

Smith stared up at the wall without answering.

"Something wrong, Smith?" asked Thomas. "You've been awfully quiet lately."

"Aw," said Ben, "he's just sad he wasn't there when the Indians attacked us! But don't worry, mate. You'll get your chance!"

"Right," said Thomas. "If any Indians show up, Smith'll take care of them!"

*   *   *

Inside his luxurious tent, Governor Ratcliffe paced back and forth, wringing his hands with worry.

"Wiggins," he complained, "we should be wallowing in riches by now. Why can't we find gold? What am I overlooking?"

There was no answer.

"Wiggins?" asked Ratcliffe, glancing round.

At that moment Wiggins came stumbling through the doorway.

"This is it, Governor, I'm done for," he moaned, and fell to the dirt floor. An arrow was sticking out of his head.

"*Indians!*" shrieked Ratcliffe.

Wiggins laughed and hopped to his feet. "Just kidding," he said. He pulled the fake arrow off his head. "See? I made it myself!"

Ratcliffe snatched the arrow.

"You idiot!" he said. Then his mouth dropped open.

"That's it!" cried Ratcliffe, waving his arms. "It's the Indians! *They* have the gold. They have it and they don't want us to take it from them. Well," he decided, "we'll just have to take it by force, won't we?" He rubbed his hands together greedily.

Ratcliffe dashed outside. "You there," he called out to Thomas, "where's Captain Smith?"

Thomas glanced round. Smith had gone. "He was just here, sir," he said. "Maybe he went off into the forest."

Ratcliffe pointed to Lon and Ben. "Well then, you there, go and find him!" he shouted.

Lon gulped. "What if we run into Indians?" he asked.

Ratcliffe glared at him. How stupid the man was!

"That's what guns are for," he told him. "Now arm yourselves and get moving!"

Just then Meeko tore out of the Governor's tent. Percy dashed out behind him, barking furiously as Meeko scurried across the settlement and ran right between Ratcliffe's legs.

Seconds later Percy sped between his master's legs too.

"What's going on here?" demanded Ratcliffe.

Wiggins appeared next, waving his arms. "That thieving black-eyed beast sneaked in and snatched some of Percy's food," he said between gasps. "And now, I'm afraid, sir, your little doggie has disappeared into the forest!"

* * *

On the other side of the forest, Indian warriors were building their own wall. They'd worked all night in the rain. By morning a stout wall of tall poles surrounded the village.

Pocahontas and Nakoma were out in a field, picking corn.

Nakoma stopped to rest. She wiped bits of corn silk from her deer skin dress.

"I'm glad the rain's stopped," she said. "But I'll be really happy when the walls are finished. I didn't sleep at all last night."

"Pocahontas," a voice called. Pocahontas turned. It was her father.

"You and Nakoma should be inside the village," Chief Powhatan told her.

"We won't be long, Father," said Pocahontas.

"We're gathering more food. It will be needed when the warriors arrive," explained Nakoma.

Chief Powhatan smiled. "That is true. But don't go far. Now is not the time to be running off."

"Yes, Father," said Pocahontas.

He looked at the necklace he had given her.

"When I see you wear that necklace, Pocahontas," he said, "you look just like your mother."

Pocahontas fingered the shiny shell. "I miss her," she said, softly. "I wish she were here."

A little breeze sprang up and rustled the corn stalks.

"She is," said Chief Powhatan, gazing at the forest. "Whenever the wind moves in the trees, I feel her presence."

He smiled at Pocahontas. "I will tell Kocoum that you are out in the cornfield," he said. "He can watch over you."

As soon as he left, Nakoma spoke.

"Pocahontas, I know you so well," she said. "You're hiding something. What is it?"

"I'm not hiding anything," said Pocahontas.

"Yes, you are," said Nakoma. "You can tell me. I promise I won't tell any…"

Then she gasped. A white man, crouching low, was coming out of the forest. He was coming straight towards them.

"What is it?" asked Pocahontas, looking round. Her heart thumped. It was John Smith!

Nakoma started to yell for help but Pocahontas quickly covered her friend's mouth. "It's all right," she said.

Shocked, Nakoma saw Pocahontas speak to the stranger.

"What are you doing here?" Pocahontas whispered.

"I wanted to see you again," Smith whispered back. "I didn't have a chance to say goodbye."

Suddenly, a man shouted from across the field. "Pocahontas!" It was Kocoum! He was heading towards them.

Pocahontas squeezed Nakoma's arm.

"Please don't say anything," she begged. She grabbed Smith's hand and while Nakoma watched in disbelief, the two fled through the rows of corn.

A few moments later, Nakoma greeted Kocoum.

"Where is Pocahontas?" he asked.

"Pocahontas?" asked Nakoma. "Let me think. I think I haven't seen her."

Kocoum gestured towards the village. "But Chief Powhatan just said she was with you."

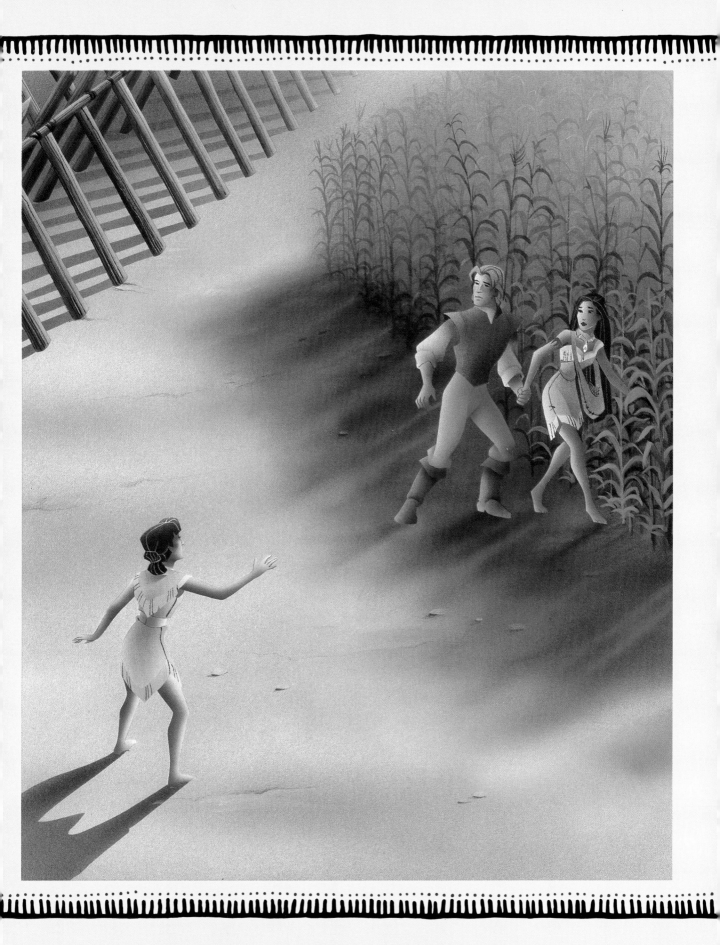

"Oh, well, yes," stammered Nakoma. "She was. But now she… isn't."

Kocoum looked suspicious. Then he spoke in an unusually gentle voice.

"Pocahontas can't keep running off," he said. "It's dangerous out there. Nakoma, you must tell her that. She listens to you."

As Kocoum walked away, Nakoma looked back at the forest. If Kocoum only knew!

* * *

Pocahontas led Smith further away from the village.

"I can't believe you came to the village," she said. "If any of the warriors had seen you…"

"Where are we going?" he asked.

"To somewhere where nobody will find us. It's my favourite place," said Pocahontas.

Pocahontas and Smith followed a winding stream that flowed into the heart of the forest. Then they stepped out into a sunny glade. In the wooded shadows, a doe and her fawn drank quietly at the stream. Beside the water stood Grandmother Willow. Smith followed Pocahontas up onto a large stump in front of the tree. Meeko climbed up behind them.

"One look at this beautiful place," Smith said, "and the men will forget all about digging for gold."

"Gold?" Pocahontas asked.

"Yes," said Smith. "That's why we're here."

"What's gold?"

Smith stopped to think. "Well," he tried to explain, "it's yellow and comes out of the ground. It is *very* valuable."

Pocahontas reached into the woven bag that hung from her shoulder. She pulled out an ear of freshly picked corn. Pulling back the husk, she pointed to the rows of shiny yellow kernels. "Here," she said, handing it to him. "We have lots of gold."

Smith smiled and tasted it.

"This is very good," he said, putting the corn into his pouch. "But it is not gold." He took a coin from his pocket. "*This* is gold."

Pocahontas studied the strange object in his hand. Meeko took the coin out of Smith's hand and bit it. Disappointed, he tossed it back and scrambled high up into the tree's branches. "There is nothing like that around here," Pocahontas said.

"Are you sure?" asked Smith.

Pocahontas nodded. "Not that I have ever seen."

"Well," said Smith, mostly to himself, "the men aren't going to like this."

Pocahontas looked relieved. "Does this mean they'll leave?"

Smith shrugged his shoulders. "I don't know. Some might."

"But what about you?" she asked. "Will you go back home – to London?"

"I don't know," answered Smith. "It's not as if I have much of a home to go back to. I guess I've never really belonged anywhere."

"You could belong here," Pocahontas said, softly.

Smith gazed high into the sweeping branches as a gentle wind rustled through the leaves. Then he gasped. Just for a moment, an old woman's face had appeared on the side of the tree! Amazed and scared, Smith sprang to his feet.

"What happened?" he asked.

Pocahontas tried not to smile. "Did you see something?"

Smith shook his head. "No, no. I just… uh… I didn't see anything – did I?"

"Look again," Pocahontas told him.

Smith stared at the tree. Slowly, before his very eyes, the old woman's face appeared again.

"Hello, John Smith," Grandmother Willow said.

Smith was almost struck speechless. "Pocahontas," he whispered, "that tree… it's… it's talking to me."

"Then you should talk back," Pocahontas whispered.

"Don't be frightened, young man," said Grandmother Willow. "My *bark* is worse than my bite."

Smith couldn't believe it. The tree was making jokes!

"Say something," Pocahontas urged him.

"What do you say to a tree?" Smith asked.

Pocahontas smiled. "Anything you like."

Smith stepped forward and took a deep breath.

"So, you, uh… live here," he stammered.

Grandmother Willow chuckled. "Come closer, John Smith."

Smith took another step.

Grandmother Willow looked at him closely.

"He has a good soul," she said to Pocahontas. "And he's handsome too."

Smith grinned and turned to Pocahontas. "I like her."

Pocahontas grinned back. "I knew you would."

"Smith!" shouted a man's voice. "Where are you? Ratcliffe's looking for you!"

"It's my men," said Smith. "We can't let them see us."

"Quick," said Grandmother Willow. "Hide behind me."

A few minutes later, Ben and Lon broke through the underbrush.

Lon glanced nervously about the open, sunny glade.

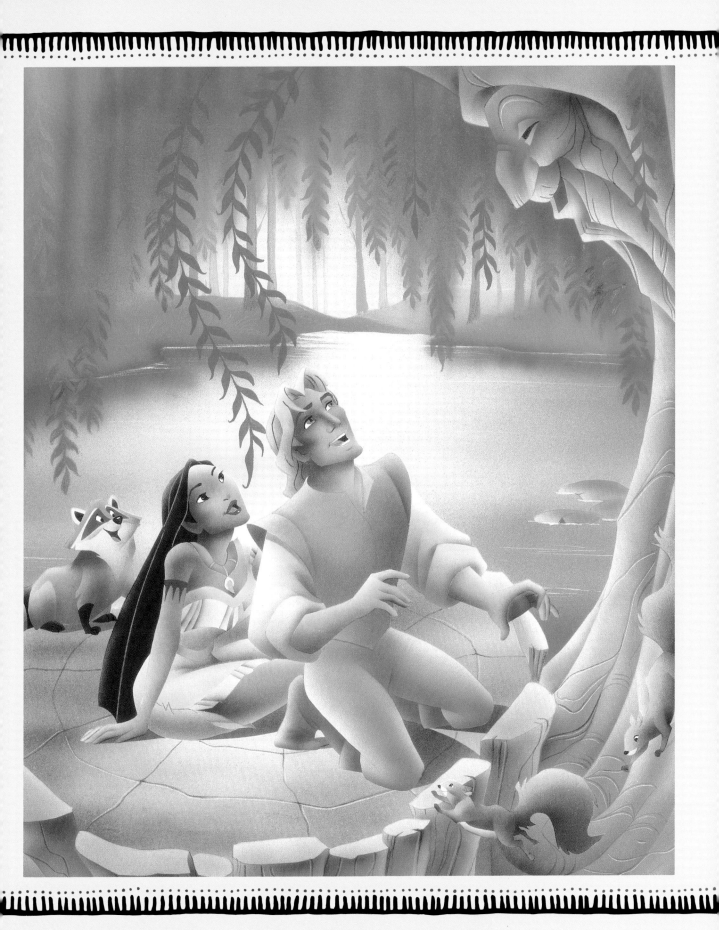

"This place gives me the creeps," he said. "Indians could be hiding here."

"Well, if you spot one," said Ben, "don't ask questions—just shoot!"

He looked up at Grandmother Willow. "Lon! Will you look at the size of this tree!"

As they stepped forward for a closer look, Ben suddenly tripped.

"Watch your feet, you big oaf," he snapped at Lon.

Lon had turned pale. "It wasn't me!" he gasped. "It was the tree. I saw it. That root just rose out of the ground—and tripped you!"

"Have you gone mad?" asked Ben. "How could a root just…"

He kicked it with his boot. Before his eyes, the root slid back underground.

"Let's get out of here!" yelled Ben.

"What about Smith?" Lon asked, running after him.

"He's a big lad," answered Ben. "He can take care of himself!"

Smith and Pocahontas came out from behind Grandmother Willow.

"I'd better get back," said Smith, "before they send the whole camp after me."

"When will I see you again?" asked Pocahontas.

"Meet me tonight," he said. "Right here."

Pocahontas nodded. "When the moon rises," she said, softly.

"I'll be waiting," Smith promised.

*   *   *

"Grandmother Willow," Pocahontas said after Smith had gone, "what am I doing? I shouldn't see him again. But I *want* to see him again."

"Who wouldn't?" asked Grandmother Willow. "*I* want to see him again!"

"I'm supposed to stay in the village," said Pocahontas. "But still, something inside is telling me it's the right thing to see him."

Grandmother Willow thought for a minute. "Perhaps it's your dream," she suggested.

"My dream…" said Pocahontas. "Grandmother Willow! Maybe he's the one the spinning arrow was pointing to!"

Grandmother Willow smiled. "It appears, my dear, that you have found your path. Listen with your heart, then you will understand."

CHAPTER EIGHT

Pocahontas ran home. When she arrived at the village she heard shouts and loud cheers coming from the river. She joined the excited crowd to see what was going on.

Warriors with painted faces, ready for battle, were paddling their long canoes towards the shore. As the warriors beached their boats, the villagers swarmed around to greet them.

Pocahontas felt someone touch her on the shoulder. It was Kocoum.

"Kocoum!" cried Pocahontas. "What is happening?"

His eyes gleamed. "Look at them! Our brothers have joined us. Now we have enough warriors to destroy those demons! The war council is gathering for a meeting," he said. "I must go now."

Pocahontas frantically searched the crowd for her father. She caught up with him just before he entered the meeting.

"Father," she pleaded, "I need to speak to you."

"Not now, my daughter," said Chief Powhatan. "The war council is gathering."

Pocahontas blocked his way. Chief Powhatan stopped in surprise.

"We don't have to fight them!" she said. "There must be a better path."

Her father looked stern. "Sometimes our paths are chosen for us," he told her.

Pocahontas tried to think fast. "But perhaps… perhaps we should try talking to them?"

Chief Powhatan frowned. "They do not want to talk."

He started to walk off.

Pocahontas grabbed his arm. "But what if one of them *did* want to talk?" she asked. "You would listen to him, wouldn't you, Father?"

"Pocahontas," the Chief began, impatiently.

"Wouldn't you?" Pocahontas persisted.

"Of course I would," he said.

Pocahontas sighed with relief.

"But it is not that simple," Chief Powhatan added. "Nothing is simple any more."

He touched Pocahontas lightly on her cheek.

"This is a very dangerous time, my daughter," he told her. "Please stay here where it is safe."

Then he went inside a nearby hut to begin the war council.

*   *   *

At the entrance gate to Jamestown, Thomas stood on sentry duty. When he heard a branch snap in the forest, he whirled round and aimed his musket.

"Easy, Thomas!" Smith called out. "It's just me!"

"Smith," said Thomas. His voice shook. "I could have killed you!"

"Not aiming like that, you couldn't," said Smith.

He took the musket, raised it to his own shoulder and aimed.

"Keep both eyes open like this when you shoot," he instructed Thomas. "You'll see twice as well."

Ben and Lon ran up to them. "Smith, there you are," said Ben. "We were looking all over for you."

Before Smith could speak, Governor Ratcliffe stormed over to him.

"*Smith!*" he shouted. "Where have you been?"

"Scouting the terrain, sir," Smith answered him.

Ratcliffe beamed. "Excellent! Then you must know the Indians' whereabouts. We'll need that information for the battle."

"What battle?" asked Smith.

"We are going to eliminate the Indians once and for all!" Ratcliffe told him.

Smith was stunned. "No, you can't do that!"

Ratcliffe narrowed his eyes. "Oh, can't I?"

"Look," said Smith, "we don't have to fight them."

Thomas' jaw dropped. "Smith, what's happened to you?"

"I met one of them," said Smith.

"You met a savage!" exclaimed Thomas.

"They're not savages," Smith said. "They can help us. They know the land, how to navigate the rivers…" He pulled the ear of corn out of his leather pouch. "And look at this!" he said. "They have food!"

Governor Ratcliffe grabbed it from him. "They don't want to feed us, they want to kill us!" he shouted. "They've got our gold and they're trying to keep it from us!"

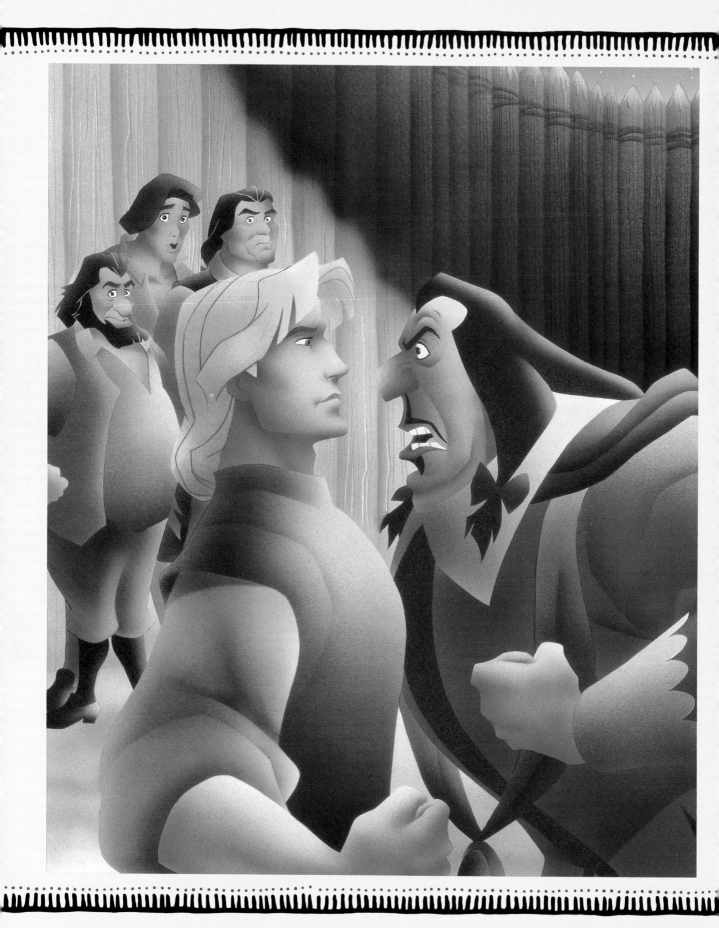

"But there *is* no gold!" Smith explained.

"No gold?" said Ben. "Then why are we here?"

"I suppose your new Indian friend told you this?" asked Ratcliffe, suspiciously.

Smith nodded.

"Lies! Lies!" yelled Ratcliffe. "There's no room for them in a civilised society!"

"But this is *their* land!" Smith broke in.

Ratcliffe shook his fist. "This is *my* land!" he shouted. "*I* make the laws here!" He stopped to think for a moment. Then he roared, "Anyone who sees an Indian must *kill* him!"

He leaned close to Smith's face. "Any man who disobeys my orders will be tried for treason and hanged."

*   *   *

Pocahontas watched the sun sink behind the trees. Soon, the moon would rise. Looking around hurriedly, she searched for a break in the wall.

Someone stepped out of the shadows. It was Nakoma. "I know what you're doing," she said. "Don't go!"

Pocahontas nervously raised a finger to her lips. "Shh!" she said. "I won't be gone long."

"I lied for you once," said Nakoma. "Don't ask me to do it again. Pocahontas, he is one of them. He's a killer!"

"You don't know him," said Pocahontas.

"How can *you* know him?" asked Nakoma. "You don't even speak his language!"

Pocahontas smiled. "We speak with our hearts," she said.

"Do not say such foolish things!" Nakoma told her. "Pocahontas, if you go out there, you'll be turning your back on your own people."

Pocahontas looked intently at her friend. "I'm trying to help my people," she said.

Nakoma sighed. It was no use.

"Pocahontas," she said, gently, "you're my friend. I don't want you to get hurt."

"I won't," said Pocahontas. "I know what I am doing."

She squeezed through a narrow opening in the wall.

"Pocahontas, no!" said Nakoma. She tried to grab her arm, but Pocahontas had already slipped away into the darkening forest.

Nakoma didn't know what to do. If she did nothing, Pocahontas might be captured, or even killed! But how could she betray her dearest friend?

Then she made up her mind. It was more important for Pocahontas to be safe! She decided to tell Kocoum and hurried back to the village.

Kocoum was outside his hut sharpening a stone knife blade. He looked up at Nakoma.

"Kocoum," she said, hesitantly. "I have something to tell you about Pocahontas. I think… she's in trouble."

As the moon rose in the sky, Nakoma told Kocoum what had happened.

*   *   *

Thomas stood quietly in the shadows and watched Smith disappear into the forest. Then he felt a heavy hand on his shoulder. Startled, he spun round and found himself face to face with Governor Ratcliffe.

"Follow him," ordered Ratcliffe. "I want to know where he's sneaking off to."

"Yes, sir," said Thomas.

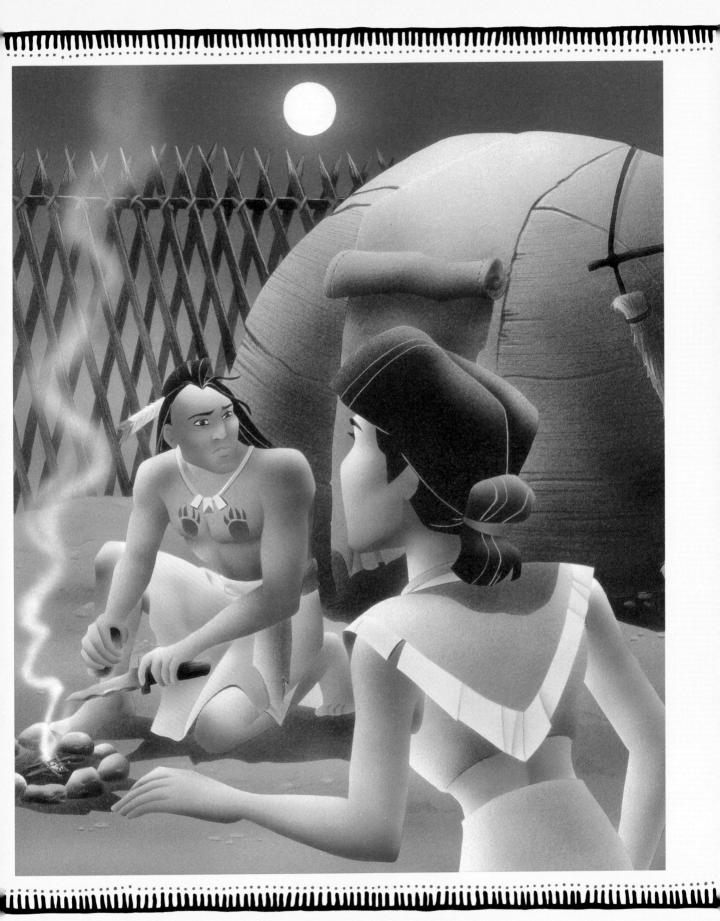

"And remember," snarled Ratcliffe. "If you happen to see any Indians—shoot them! You've been a slipshod sailor and a poor excuse for a soldier. Don't disappoint me again!"

*   *   *

Pocahontas ran into the moonlit glade.

"What's happening, child?" asked Grandmother Willow. "I feel the earth is trembling with fear."

At that moment, Smith came into sight.

As soon as Pocahontas saw him, she ran into his arms.

"Pocahontas," Smith said, "listen to me. We don't have much time. My men are planning to attack your village. You've got to warn them."

Pocahontas was stunned by the news. "Our village is filled with warriors. They are planning to attack *your* people!"

She took Smith's hand and began to pull him. "Before it's too late," she said, "you have to come with me and talk to my father."

"Your father?" asked Smith.

Pocahontas nodded. "He said he'd talk to anyone who comes in peace."

"It's not that easy," Smith told her. "I don't think talking is going to do any good."

"But we have to do *something*!" said Pocahontas.

Smith shook his head sadly. "I've already tried talking to my men. It's no use."

Suddenly, a muffled howl came from the forest. Pocahontas turned to see Meeko and Flit emerge from the underbrush. Staggering behind them was Percy, his head stuck in a small log. Exhausted, the little dog fell in a heap.

"That's the strangest creature I've ever seen," remarked Grandmother Willow.

"Percy!" said Smith, freeing him from the log. "Are you all right?"

As soon as Percy was unstuck, he scrambled to his feet, growled and sprang after Meeko. Wildly, the animals chased each other round and round Grandmother Willow.

"Meeko!" scolded Pocahontas. "Stop it! What are you doing?"

Smith lunged at Percy, finally chasing him onto Grandmother Willow's stump. "You see what I mean?" said Smith. "We can't even stop two little animals from fighting. How do you expect us to stop two armies?"

Grandmother Willow spoke up. "I can't believe I'm hearing this," she said.

Smith and Pocahontas looked up in surprise.

"Come over here," said Grandmother Willow. She reached down and dipped one of her branches into the water. "Look!"

Smith peered into the moonlit stream. "I don't see anything."

"The ripples," said Pocahontas, looking closely.

"Yes," said Grandmother Willow. "So small at first, then look how they grow." She nudged Smith with a branch. "But *someone* has to start them."

Smith leaned over and studied the widening rings of water.

"And that someone is us," Smith said, looking up at Grandmother Willow.

"Pocahontas," Smith said, standing up straight. "Let's go and talk to your father."

Pocahontas threw her arms round Smith's neck and kissed him.

Suddenly, Kocoum, shrieking a fierce war cry, crashed through the glade and sprang at Smith. Caught off balance, Smith fell to the ground. Pocahontas cried out in horror as Kocoum pulled out his knife.

Smith grabbed the furious warrior's hand and shoved him away. But Kocoum lunged at Smith again.

"Kocoum, no!" cried Pocahontas.

At that moment Thomas ran into the glade. Seeing the fight, he raised his musket, closed one eye and took careful aim.

"Both eyes open," he reminded himself. He opened both eyes. Then he fired.

Kocoum clutched his chest and sank to his knees.

Smith spun round. "Thomas!" he gasped. Pocahontas ran to Kocoum's side and tried to support him.

As Kocoum slipped to the ground, his hand caught in Pocahontas' necklace, tearing it from her neck.

"You killed him!" Pocahontas cried at Thomas. "You killed Kocoum!"

Thomas started to move towards Kocoum. "I didn't mean… He was trying… I thought that…"

Pocahontas rushed towards Thomas. "Get away from him!"

"He was only trying to protect me," Smith said, trying to hold her back.

"He killed him!" sobbed Pocahontas.

Then the sound of war cries filled the forest, growing louder and louder.

"Thomas," ordered Smith, "get out of here!"

Thomas, pale with shock, stared at Kocoum's lifeless body.

"*Get out of here!*" Smith roared at him.

His eyes stinging with tears, Thomas bolted into the trees.

Moments later the moonlit glade swarmed with warriors. Seeing Kocoum's body, their eyes filled with fury. Four of them seized Smith, tied his hands and dragged him away.

The other warriors gently lifted Kocoum's body. Hoisting him high above their shoulders, they carried their dead comrade back home.

Grief-stricken, Pocahontas sank to the ground, stunned at all that had happened. After the last warrior's voice faded, she rose and slowly walked back home. Side by side, Meeko and Percy followed sadly behind.

CHAPTER NINE

hief Powhatan felt his heart break. He stood under the stars as the warriors placed Kocoum's body at his feet. His face looked hard as stone.

"Who did this?" he demanded.

The warriors pushed Smith forward.

"Pocahontas was out in the forest. Kocoum went to find her," one of them said. "This white man attacked them."

Chief Powhatan looked straight into Smith's eyes.

"Your weapons are strong," he told him. "But now our anger is stronger."

Then, in the fading moonlight, he addressed the grieving villagers.

"At sunrise," Chief Powhatan roared, "he will be the first to die."

As the warriors started to drag Smith away, Pocahontas ran up to her father.

"Father, wait!" she cried.

Chief Powhatan spun round and took her aside. "Pocahontas," he said. "I told you to stay in the village. You disobeyed me! You have shamed me!"

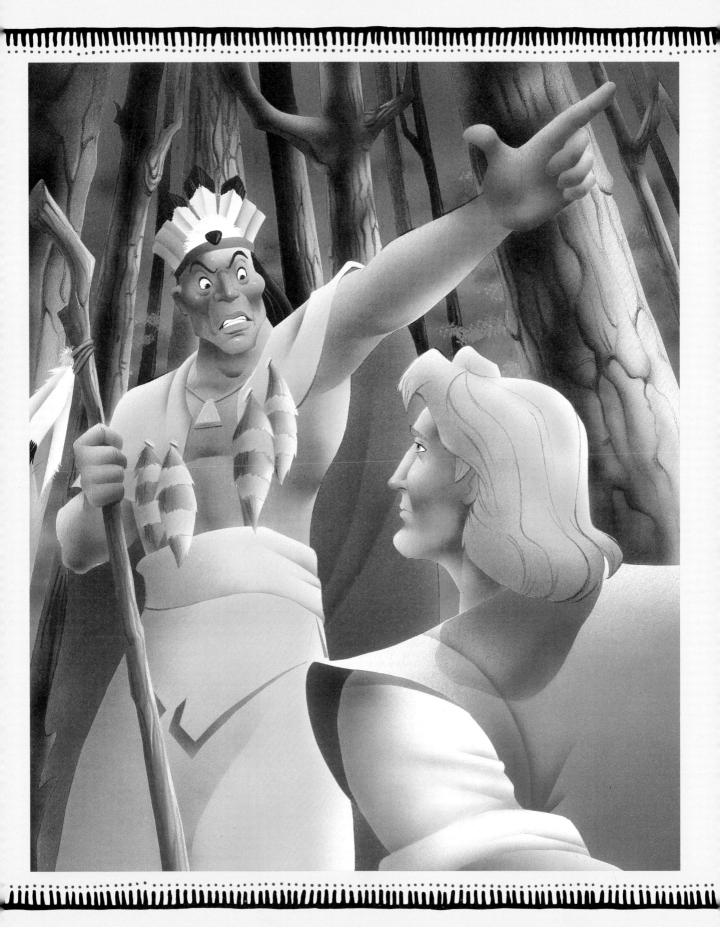

"But Father," Pocahontas tried to explain, "I was only trying to help."

"Because of your foolishness," said Chief Powhatan, "Kocoum is dead."

Pocahontas felt crushed by his words. What he said was awful and true. She knew he would hear nothing else she had to say.

"Take the prisoner away!" ordered Chief Powhatan.

Pocahontas couldn't bear to watch. Nakoma came out of the crowd and put her arm round her friend.

"I should have stayed in the village," Pocahontas told her, wiping her eyes.

"It's not your fault," said Nakoma.

"Yes, it is," said Pocahontas. "Kocoum was just coming to protect me. If I hadn't gone out there…"

"No, Pocahontas," said Nakoma. Her voice was shaking. "I sent Kocoum after you."

"What?" gasped Pocahontas.

"I was so worried," said Nakoma. "I didn't want you to get hurt. I thought I was doing the right thing."

Pocahontas gently touched her friend's cheek. "You were," she said. "All this happened because of me. And now Smith is going to die." Pocahontas' eyes were brimming with tears. "I need to see him, Nakoma," she said, "one last time."

Nakoma took Pocahontas by the hand. "Come with me," she said. "I know where they took him."

She led Pocahontas across the village to a secluded hut.

Two guards at the doorway stopped them.

Nakoma spoke up. "Pocahontas wants to look into the eyes of the man who killed Kocoum."

The guards, uncertain, looked at each other.

"Are you going to deny the wishes of the daughter of the Chief?" Nakoma asked them.

They stepped aside and let Pocahontas in.

Smith was sitting on the ground, tied to a post. The tiny room was lit by a torch stuck into the dirt floor.

"Pocahontas!" he said, surprised to see her.

Pocahontas threw her arms round his neck. "I'm so sorry," she whispered.

"For what?" said Smith. He tried to smile. "I've got out of worse scrapes than this. Can't think of any right now, but…"

Tears streamed down Pocahontas' face. "It would have been better if we had never met," she said. "None of this would have happened."

"Pocahontas, look at me," Smith said. "I had to meet you. Because if I hadn't, I'd still be the man I was."

"What do you mean?" asked Pocahontas.

"You've changed me," Smith told her. "If I had never known you, I would never have known how precious life can be."

Pocahontas wiped away her tears.

"I was so foolish," she said. "I thought our love could make the whole world bright." She shook her head sadly. "I never knew that fear and hate could be so strong. But still, my heart knows that we were right."

Nakoma poked her head inside the hut. "We had better go."

Pocahontas sobbed and clutched Smith's sleeve. "I can't leave you."

"You never will," he said. "No matter what happens to me. I'll always be with you. *Forever.*"

* * *

Thomas stumbled wildly from the moonlit forest.

"Help!" he shouted, bursting through the settlement gate. "Somebody, help! Help! Help!"

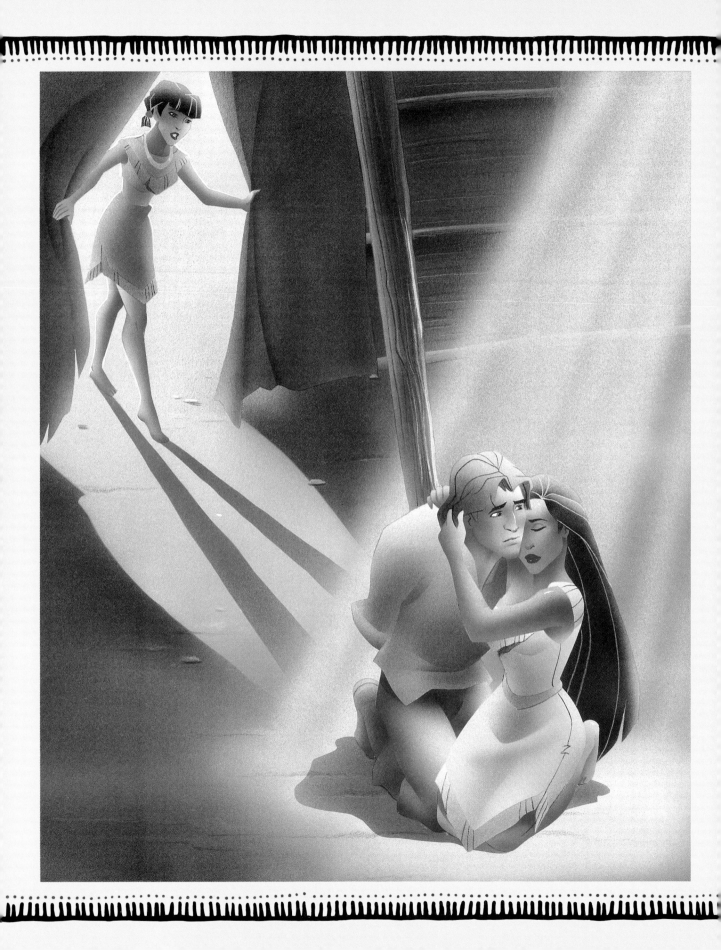

Carrying a lantern, Lon came running up to him. "Easy, lad. What is it?"

While more men clustered about him, Thomas stopped to catch his breath. Then he cried out, "It's Smith! The Indians got him! Captured him. Carried him off!"

"How many were there?" asked Ben. "Where'd they take him?"

"They headed north," Thomas told him. "There were at least a dozen of them."

Lon shook his fist. "Ratcliffe was right. They *are* savages!"

"We've got to save him!" cried Thomas. "He'd do the same for any of us."

"He's right," said Ben. "We've got to do something."

Overhearing the commotion, Governor Ratcliffe came out of his tent.

"It's perfect, Wiggins," he whispered. "I couldn't have planned this better myself. The gold is as good as mine!"

Ratcliffe strode up to the men. "And so we *shall* rescue Smith!" he boomed. "I told you those Indians couldn't be trusted. Smith tried to befriend them and look what they've done!"

Ratcliffe unsheathed his sword and held it high.

"It's time to rescue our courageous comrade!" he cried into the night. "Gather your weapons. At daybreak we attack!"

* * *

In his village not far away, Chief Powhatan had just cried out those very same words.

CHAPTER TEN

hile it was still dark, Pocahontas paddled towards the heart of the forest. As soon as the canoe slid into the glade, she leapt out and ran to Grandmother Willow.

"They're going to kill Smith at sunrise!" she cried.

Grandmother Willow was horrified. "You have to stop them!" she said.

Pocahontas put her hands to her mouth and shook her head. "I can't."

"Child," said Grandmother Willow, "you must not turn away from your path. Remember your dream."

"I don't know *which* way to turn," sobbed Pocahontas. "I feel so lost."

Just then, Meeko raced up into a tree. In a moment he was at Pocahontas' side, nudging her arm. He was holding something shiny – Smith's compass.

Pocahontas smiled, sadly. "Thank you, Meeko," she said, taking it from him. In the dim light she watched the needle spin and remembered Smith's words, "It tells you how to find your way when you get lost…"

Pocahontas stopped short. She noticed something for the first time. The needle was shaped like a tiny arrow.

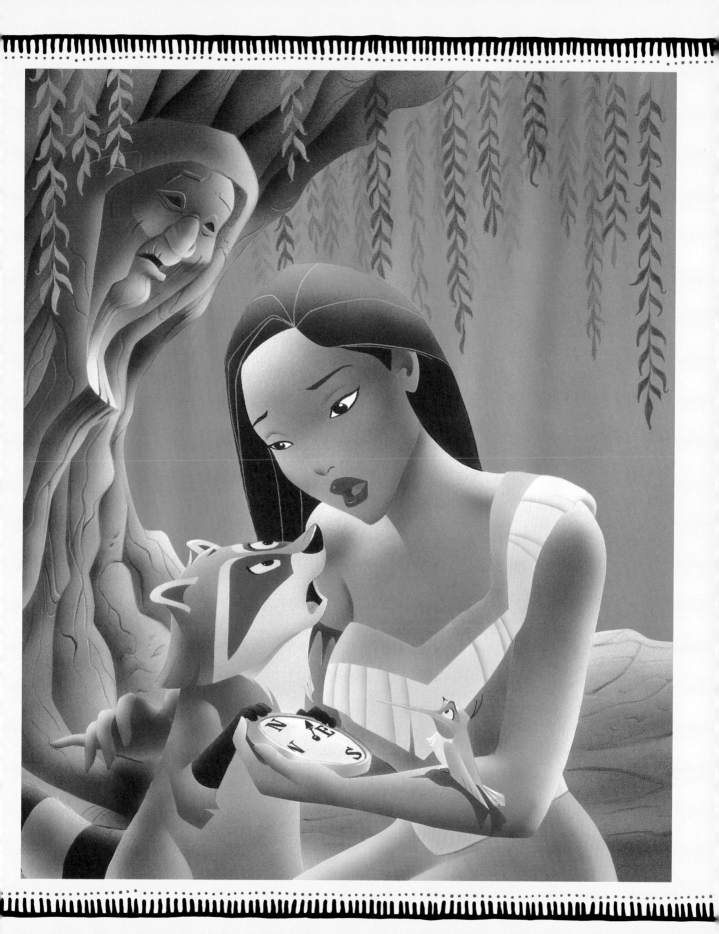

"Spinning arrow," she breathed, her excitement growing.

"It's the arrow from your dream," said Grandmother Willow.

"I was right!" Pocahontas cried. "This *is* my path!"

The compass face glinted in the first rays of early light. Pocahontas looked to the glowing eastern sky. The sun was rising.

"It's sunrise!" she gasped. "I'm too late!"

"Have faith, child," said Grandmother Willow. "Let the spirits of the earth guide you."

As Pocahontas gazed up at Grandmother Willow, a gentle wind began to blow. It ruffled Pocahontas' hair. Feeling its comforting presence around her, Pocahontas thought of her mother and smiled.

Quickly the wind picked up speed and the compass needle began to spin wildly. It spun faster and faster. Then all at once it stopped.

"It's pointing east," said Pocahontas, "to the sunrise!"

As swift as a lightning bolt, the wind cleared an opening for her through the forest.

"You know your path, child," said Grandmother Willow. "Now follow it!"

Pocahontas raced through the shadowy trees. As she ran, the wind stayed with her — pushing steadily at her back. There was so little time. She had to get home before it was too late.

*   *   *

Governor Ratcliffe stood at attention in the centre of Jamestown. Smiling broadly, he watched the rim of gold peep above the horizon. The day had come at last — the day they would wipe out the Indians. And, while they were at it, if they managed to rescue Smith — well, that would be good too.

Ratcliffe turned to face his battalion of waiting men.

"Onward!" he ordered, waving his sword in the air.

At once the settlers marched into the forest, hacking at the trees and bushes that stood in their way.

* * *

Atop a high plateau, Chief Powhatan was watching the rising sun too. He knew the sun was dawning on his people's brightest day – the day of their victory over the invaders!

But first there was something else to attend to.

He turned to the villagers. They were all standing in a semicircle near the plateau's edge. In the centre of the circle lay a stone slab.

"Bring out the prisoner," Chief Powhatan demanded.

Two warriors brought Smith out. They pushed him onto the stone slab and held him down. Chief Powhatan raised his war club.

At that moment Ratcliffe and his men burst out of the trees at the foot of the plateau and raised their muskets.

"*No!*" cried Pocahontas, racing past them.

She ran up to her father and threw herself across Smith's body to protect him.

Ratcliffe's men halted, frozen with shock.

Astounded, Chief Powhatan lowered his arm. "Pocahontas!"

She looked up at him. "If you kill him," she said, "you'll have to kill me too."

"Daughter!" ordered the Chief. "Stand back!"

"I won't," Pocahontas said, still holding onto Smith. "I love him, Father."

Chief Powhatan was stunned.

"Look around you," said Pocahontas. "This is where the path of hatred has brought us."

Chief Powhatan could see the white men positioned at the edge of the forest. His own warriors, arrows poised in their bows, were looking to him for orders.

"This is the path *I* choose, Father. What will yours be?" said Pocahontas.

As she spoke, the wind stirred in the surrounding trees. Leaves of green, scarlet and gold floated about everyone's head. As the wind swirled gently around Chief Powhatan's shoulders, his eyes grew misty. Then, standing tall, he raised his voice for all to hear.

"My daughter speaks with a wisdom beyond her years," he said. "We have all come here with anger in our hearts. But she comes with courage and understanding. It is that spirit that will guide us to a place of peace."

He turned to his warriors.

"Release the prisoner!" he demanded.

All the warriors, stirred by the power of their Chief's words, lowered their weapons.

At that, Governor Ratcliffe yelled, "Now's our chance, men! Fire!"

Thomas, moved by the warriors' actions, immediately stepped forward and lowered his musket. One by one, his comrades followed.

"Fine," said Ratcliffe. "I'll settle this myself."

Before anyone could move, Ratcliffe grabbed a musket and aimed straight at Chief Powhatan.

In an instant Smith threw himself at Chief Powhatan and knocked him out of the way. But Ratcliffe had already pulled the trigger. The musket fired and Smith fell to the ground.

"He's shot Smith!" cried Thomas.

Enraged, Ratcliffe's men closed in on him.

"Put him in chains!" shouted Thomas.

The angry men grabbed Ratcliffe.

"Smith stepped right into it!" the Governor protested. "It's his own fault. You saw it yourself." He broke away from their grasp and ran, tripping over Meeko and Percy.

"I'll see that you are all hanged for this!" Ratcliffe shouted as they recaptured him and put him in chains.

"Gag him as well," added Thomas. He hurried over to Smith's side. Pocahontas, crying softly, was holding him in her arms. He was still alive.

CHAPTER ELEVEN

n less than a week the *Susan Constant* was loaded and ready for the voyage back to England.

Just before the ship set sail, Thomas helped to carry Smith down to the shore. Gently the men placed the stretcher in a shady spot under the trees.

Smith smiled weakly at Thomas.

"I'm glad you're staying behind," he said. "When the new settlers arrive, you can help..." Then Smith began to cough.

"I'll get you some water," Thomas said.

He hurried over to a rain barrel and filled the tin dipper. Ben and Lon joined him.

"How's Smith holding up?" asked Ben.

"He should be all right," said Thomas, "as long as he gets back to England."

A commotion erupted near the settlement gate.

"Look," said Lon, "here they come with Ratcliffe."

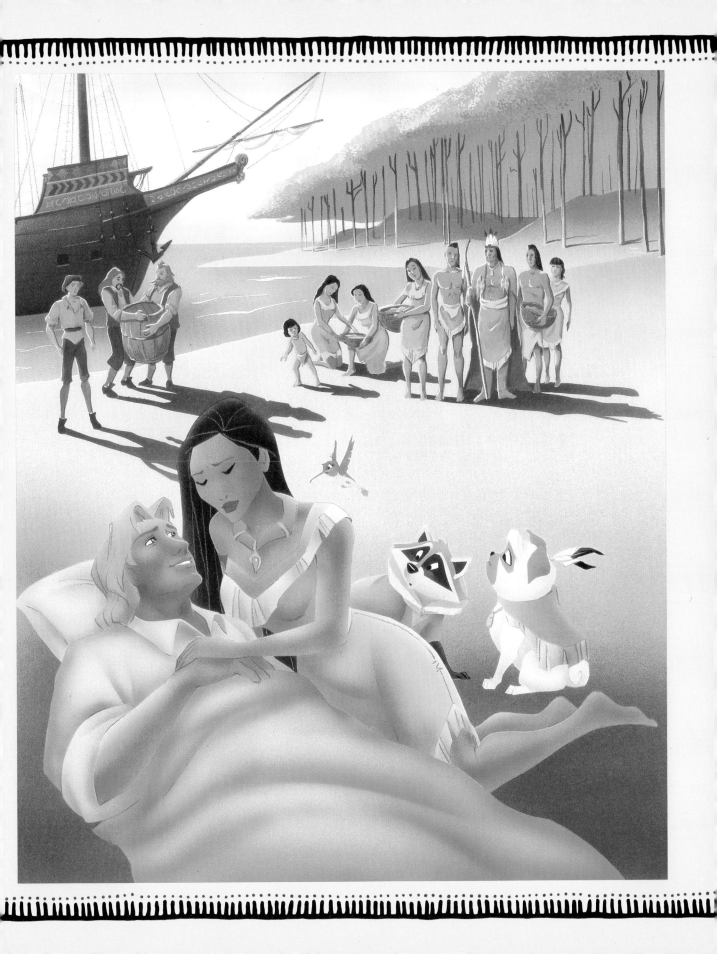

The Governor struggled vainly with his chains while he was hustled into a small boat and rowed out to the ship.

Thomas held Smith's head up while he drank.

"Make sure you tell them back home what has happened here," said Thomas.

Smith nodded. "I will."

"We'd better get you on board," said Ben, "before the tide goes out."

Smith held up his hand. "No, not yet. Pocahontas said she'd be here."

Wincing, he pushed himself up on his elbow and looked towards the forest. Then he smiled. "She's coming," he said, falling back on the stretcher. "Thomas, go and meet her."

Pocahontas had reached the edge of the clearing. Chief Powhatan and Nakoma were at her side.

"Does he have to go?" Pocahontas asked Thomas.

"Going back is his only chance," Thomas said, kindly. "He'll die if he stays here."

For several moments Pocahontas stared out at the river. Nakoma put her arm round her.

"I know what you are thinking," she said. "But remember, dear Pocahontas, the fighting has stopped because of you. Who knows what will happen if you leave?"

Pocahontas watched her people coming from the village. They were carrying blankets and baskets of corn for the white men. *This is the first peace since the sailing ship arrived*, she thought.

She went to Smith. Kneeling, Pocahontas stroked his forehead.

"I have something for you," she said. Pocahontas tucked a small leather pouch into his shirt. "It is powdered bark from Grandmother Willow. It will help with the pain."

"What pain?" asked Smith. "I've had worse pain than this. Can't think of when right now, but…" Then he shivered.

Chief Powhatan removed his cloak and laid it over Smith.

Smith smiled. "Thank you," he said.

Flit buzzed over and alighted on Smith's finger.

"I thought you didn't like strangers," said Smith, weakly.

He watched as Meeko and Percy scrambled up to Pocahontas and dropped something in her lap.

"My mother's necklace!" said Pocahontas. "Thank you."

Smith patted the two animals and smiled.

"Will you come with me?" he asked Pocahontas, taking her hand.

Pocahontas looked up at her father.

"You must choose your own path," he told her.

Tears streamed down Pocahontas' face.

Smith knew her decision. She had to stay and help to keep the peace between the two nations and told Smith so. "Then I will stay here with you," Smith said.

Pocahontas shook her head. "No," she said. "You have to go back."

"But I can't leave you," said Smith.

"You will never leave me," Pocahontas said. "No matter what happens, I'll always be with you. *Forever*."

* * *

Pocahontas ran to the edge of a cliff. Alone, she watched as the *Susan Constant* moved away from her, its huge white sails billowing in the wind. Slowly moving her hand in a circle, she said goodbye as the ship moved further down the wide river to the waters that had no end.